Aoife

# Hansel and Gretel

illustrated by Andrea Petrlik

**Child's Play (International) Ltd**
Ashworth Rd, Bridgemead, Swindon, SN5 7YD UK
Swindon          Auburn ME          Sydney
© 2005 Child's Play (International) Ltd    Printed in Heshan, China
ISBN 978-1-904550-73-0          L150714FUFT0914730
13 15 17 19 20 18 16 14 12
www.childs-play.com

A woodcutter lived in a large forest with his wife and two children, called Hansel and Gretel. The family was very poor, and there was no money to buy food for them all.

"We cannot afford to feed the children," said the woodcutter's wife.
"You must take them into the forest and leave them there."
"How can I do that to them?" asked the woodcutter.
"They will be eaten by wolves!"
"You must," said his wife,
"or we will all starve."

Hansel and Gretel
were too hungry to sleep,
and overheard their parents.
"Don't worry," said Gretel.
"I have a plan!"

The next day, the children's father gave them each
a lump of bread, and took them deep into the forest.

Gretel dropped crumbs
behind them as they walked.
"So that we can find
our way back again,"
she whispered to Hansel.

When they reached the middle of the wood, the woodcutter told the children to sit down. "I'm going to cut wood," he explained. "Wait here until I fetch you."

The children waited and waited, but their father never came back.

When night started to fall, Gretel turned
to her brother. "Right," she said. "Time to go
before the wolves come out!"
But when the children began to follow
the trail of breadcrumbs, they found
that all the hungry creatures
of the forest had already
eaten them.

"Oh no," Gretel started to cry.
"Now we will never find our way home."

"Don't worry," Hansel comforted her.
"As long as we stay together, we will be
all right.  Let's follow this little path.
It looks as though someone has passed
this way recently."

They followed the path a little way,
until it opened into a hidden
clearing.  In the middle of
the clearing was a house.

What an amazing house it was,
built completely out of food!
The roof was made of chocolate,
and the walls of gingerbread.
Everything was decorated
with candies, cookies
and icing.

The hungry children fell
upon the house, breaking
off small pieces and cramming
them in their mouths.

Suddenly, an old woman appeared.
"Why are you children eating my house?" she asked,
"When there is plenty of food inside?"

She welcomed them in, and gave
them a feast fit for a king.
"You must sleep here tonight," she said.
"I will take you home in the morning."

"I told you we'd be safe," said Hansel.
"We'll be back home tomorrow.
And perhaps we can even ask to take
some food for our parents."

But in the morning, Hansel was woken
by the old woman dragging him to a small hut.
She threw him in, locked the door
and hung the key on a high hook.
"I'll feed and feed you," she cackled.
"And when you're fat enough, I'll have such a feast!"

Then she woke Gretel, roughly.
"Wake up, lazybones!" she said.
"There's work to do in the kitchen."
She made Gretel work all day,
cooking food for Hansel to eat,
but she would not let Gretel eat anything herself.

Luckily, Hansel saved some food
for his sister, and gave it to her
when the old woman was not looking.

After a couple of days, the old woman wanted
to see if Hansel was fat enough to eat.

"Poke your finger out," she ordered.
"Let's see how much fat you've put on."
Hansel poked out an old chicken bone
instead of his finger.
"That's too thin,"
the old woman complained.
"You're not ready to eat yet.
I suppose I'll have to wait."

Time passed.
Hansel grew fatter,
and Gretel too.

But every time the
old woman wanted to
see if Hansel was ready
to eat, he stuck out
the same chicken bone.

Before long, though, she could not wait any more,
and she made Gretel light the oven.
"I don't care if he's not ready yet," she said.
"I am hungry for meat!" And she told
Gretel to get in the oven to see
if it was hot enough.

"I don't know how," said Gretel. "Will you show me?"
"Silly goose!" said the old woman.
"Like this!"

The minute the old woman
leant into the oven,
Gretel pushed her
all the way in,
and slammed
the door shut.

She grabbed the key
to Hansel's hut and let him out.
Before they escaped, they looked through
the house to make sure there were
no other captives.

There was no one else there, but they did find
a little box of jewels taken from other people
the old woman had imprisoned.

Gretel put this in her pocket,
and the two children ran into
the forest. They wandered
for hours, lost, until
suddenly they heard
the sound of trees
being chopped.

"Father! Father!" they shouted,
and ran towards the sound.
They found their father cutting down trees.

"It's a miracle!" he said.
"I thought you were dead!
How I have missed you!
I sent my wife away
after what she
made me do."

The two children hugged their father,
and he promised never to let them go again,
however poor they might be.

"Let's go home and celebrate," he continued,
"even though there is still no food to eat."

"Never mind about that," laughed Gretel,
pulling out the box of jewels.

"With these, we can buy
all the food and drink we will
ever need for the rest of our lives!"